S0-DBC-414

SEATTLE

M I C H A E L   E .   G O O D M A N

T H E   H I S T O R Y   O F   T H E

MARINERS

C R E A T I V E   E D U C A T I O N

Published by Creative Education
123 South Broad Street, Mankato, Minnesota 56001
Creative Education is an imprint of The Creative Company

Designed by Rita Marshall
Editorial assistance by Neal Bernards & John Nichols

Photos by: Allsport Photography, Focus on Sports, Fotosport, SportsChrome.

Printed in the United States of America.

Library of Congress Cataloging-in-Publication Data

Goodman, Michael.
The History of the Seattle Mariners / by Michael Goodman.
p. cm. — (Baseball)
Summary: A team history of the Seattle Mariners, a club formed in 1976 with the awarding of an American League franchise to Seattle.
ISBN: 0-88682-925-9

1. Seattle Mariners (Baseball team)—History—Juvenile literature.
[1. Seattle Mariners (Baseball team)—History. 2. Baseball—History.]
I. Title. II. Series: Baseball (Mankato, Minn.)

GV875.S42G66 1999
796.357'64'09797772—dc21 97-6342

First edition

9 8 7 6 5 4 3 2 1

Rain descends in a mist on the Pacific Northwest. It falls from clouds that sweep in from the ocean, feeding the streams, bays, and rivers around Seattle, Washington. Sailboats of all shapes and colors glide on the bays, inlets, and coves of Puget Sound surrounding the city. Thousands of sailors, also called mariners, ply the waters for their work and recreation. When it came time to name the city's new major league baseball team in 1976, Seattle fans thought it only fitting to call the ballclub the "Mariners."

Today, the Seattle Mariners are a successful team led by four amazing players: outfielder Ken Griffey Jr., a home-run

Tommy Harper, a member of the original Seattle Pilots.

hitting slugger who enjoys chasing down fly balls as much as knocking them out of the park; lanky pitcher Randy "Big Unit" Johnson, whose fastball is the most feared in baseball; designated hitter Edgar Martinez, whose consistency at the plate has earned him two batting titles; and newcomer Alex Rodriguez, a hot-hitting young shortstop who is already at the top of his game.

The Pilots left for Milwaukee after playing just one season in old Ranier Stadium.

In the past, however, the Mariners have given Seattle baseball fans little to cheer about. In fact, Seattle's first winning season didn't occur until 1991. And it wasn't until 1995 that the fans' patience was rewarded when the Mariners reached the American League playoffs for the first time. It had been a long, slow road to those postseason games, but for the Mariners' faithful, it was worth the wait.

STRUGGLING AT THE START

Believe it or not, winning games wasn't even the biggest challenge at first for Seattle baseball players and fans. The initial problem was just getting and keeping a major-league team in the "Emerald City," as Seattle is often called for its lush green beauty. For many years, local fans were content to root for the minor-league Seattle Rainiers of the Pacific Coast League. Then, in 1968, major league baseball finally came to Seattle when a club called the Pilots joined the American League. Unfortunately, that franchise had money problems and lasted only one season. The next year, the Pilots' owners sold the club to a Wisconsin group, which moved the team to Milwaukee and renamed it the Brewers.

Seattle baseball fans didn't give up hope, however. In

A Mariners power threat, Edgar Martinez.

Wilson

February of 1976, the American League announced that a new franchise had been awarded to Seattle, and the team would begin play the following season. The new club would also have a new home—the King County Domed Stadium, or "Kingdome" for short. The stadium could seat nearly 60,000 fans under a Teflon roof that would protect against Seattle's rainy and often chilly summer weather.

1 9 7 7

Glenn Abbott led the Mariners by winning seven consecutive starts—a team record that stood until 1984.

Seattle had a team, a name, and a new stadium, and now it needed players. A special draft was held after the 1976 season so the Mariners could pick players from the rosters of the established American League squads.

Excitement began to build in Seattle for Opening Night, April 6, 1977. Manager Darrell Johnson announced that Diego Segui would pitch the new team's first game. Mariners fans thought Segui was the perfect choice since the Cuban right-hander had also been the best hurler for the old Seattle Pilots. He is the only player ever to pitch for both Seattle teams. Nearly 58,000 noisy supporters jammed the Kingdome to see if Segui could shut down the California Angels. He couldn't. The Mariners lost their first game 7–0. Two nights later, however, Bill Laxton recorded the team's first victory, a 7–6 comeback win over the Angels.

For the rest of that first season, the Mariners continued their up-and-down play. They would win one night and then lose the next game or two. By year's end, they had achieved a 64–98 record, finishing in sixth place.

Still, fans were not discouraged. They had watched several exciting offensive players lead their team. For example, outfielder Lee Stanton smacked 27 home runs and drove in 90 runs. Rookie Ruppert Jones led the club in doubles and triples and slugged 24 homers. He was also named to the American League All-Star team. Whenever he would come to bat, the Kingdome would resound with shouts of "Rupe! Rupe!" from adoring fans.

BOCHTE LEADS THE ATTACK

In the early years, Bruce Bochte was the Mariners' most consistent hitter, as well as the Seattle club's first real star. He joined the Mariners as a free agent in 1978 after playing for several other American League teams. From the very beginning of his career, Bochte had all of the tools to be a great player. When veteran major-league manager Dick Williams first saw Bochte perform, he predicted, "With his swing, his desire, his concentration, and his ability to consistently get a piece of almost every pitch, this kid is a natural to win a batting championship."

Bochte's first year in Seattle went well. He started out the 1978 season with a hitting streak and was batting above .300 in May. Then he began pressing. "I expected to win games single-handedly," he recalled. "In the beginning, I was the only one on the team hitting the ball. It got to the point that I felt that if I didn't get two hits and drive in two runs, we wouldn't win the game." That pressure became mental torture. By season's end, Bochte's average had dropped to a mediocre .263, and he had driven in only 51 runs. Bochte's batting slump during the last few months of the season was one of the reasons Seattle fell to last place in 1978.

Bochte and the Mariners were determined to improve in 1979. The team acquired veteran Willie Horton, one of the

1979

Willie Horton hit his 300th career homer, becoming only the 43rd player to do so.

A lefty star of the '80s, Mark Langston.

First baseman Alvin Davis.

American League's best home-run hitters, to bat behind Bochte in the Seattle lineup. Now the Mariners had fleet second baseman Julio Cruz leading off and stealing bases, and Bochte and Horton batting third and fourth and driving in runs. Ruppert Jones and Dan Meyer were also on hand to provide still more offensive punch.

1 9 8 1

Rene Lachemann replaced Maury Wills as Seattle's skipper, becoming the third manager in team history.

All of this extra support in the lineup helped Bochte have his best year ever in 1979. The smooth-swinging left-hander kept his average above .300 throughout the season and finished the year hitting .316 and driving in 100 runs, both Seattle club records at the time. "This is the most fun I ever had," Bochte said. "It came from learning how to relax and take things as they come."

The highlight of the year for Bochte and Mariners fans came on July 17, when Seattle hosted the 50th All-Star Game at the Kingdome. Bochte was selected as an All-Star and knocked in a go-ahead run for the American League. However, his teammates could not hold the lead, and the National League won 7–6. Despite the loss, Bochte had given Seattle fans a thrill.

Bochte had several more fine years for the Mariners. Then, after the 1982 season, he decided to retire from baseball because the game was no longer fun for him. Mariners fans were sad to see their first real hero go.

BALL-DOCTORING CONTROVERSY

While early Seattle teams featured such good hitters as Bruce Bochte, Willie Horton, and Ruppert Jones, the club lacked solid pitching. As a result, the Mariners had lots of trouble winning during their first 15 years in the majors. No matter how many runs the offense could produce, the pitchers seemed to give up more.

The Seattle owners decided to add an experienced starter in 1982 to lead their young pitchers. So Mariners management signed one of the game's oldest and craftiest stars, Gaylord Perry. Perry, a 20-year veteran, was a crowd favorite who had a reputation for loading up the ball with spit or grease before he pitched.

1 9 8 2

Mariners ace Floyd Bannister led the team in wins (12) and innings pitched (247).

No one could be sure whether Perry really threw spitballs, but he liked to make batters think he did. He would go through a ritual before each pitch. First he would wipe his pitching hand across his sweaty brow. Next, he would drag his fingers along the brim of his hat to make hitters think he kept Vaseline there. Then he would rub the ball carefully before going into his windup. All of this activity drove batters nuts—which was exactly what Perry wanted.

Perry came into the 1982 season with 297 career victories, needing just three more wins to become the 14th 300-game winner in baseball history. After collecting two wins in April, nearly 30,000 fans poured into the Kingdome for Perry's May 7 start to see if he would enter the history books.

The Mariners' batters gave Perry a quick 5–0 lead, so it was up to Gaylord himself to preserve the win. He kept New York Yankees hitters off-balance throughout the game. At the end of the 7–3 victory, excited Mariner fans gave the wily veteran a standing ovation.

Ken Kaiser, who was umpiring that night, said, "Gaylord's fastball was as good as I've ever seen him throw it. He kept the ball down, and that forkball of his was popping."

1 9 8 4

Rookie of the Year runner-up Mark Langston led Seattle in victories (17), ERA (3.40), and innings pitched (225).

The Mariners' strong performance in 1982 was just the start of a decade of improvement in Seattle. The team began to develop some good pitching, and the best of the bunch was young southpaw Mark Langston.

Langston had 17 victories in 1984 and became the first rookie since Herb Score in 1955 to lead the American League in strikeouts.

Amazingly, Langston was almost demoted to the minors in midseason. In the early part of the year, he had relied almost entirely on his fastball to get batters out. That worked in the minors, but unfortunately for the young pitcher, he couldn't overpower the more experienced American League hitters. Then one day, Seattle pitching coach Frank Funk saw Langston throwing a slow, sharp-breaking curveball during practice. He asked the young hurler to try that pitch during his next start. By mixing the fastball and his curve, Langston struck out nine batters in seven innings and won the contest. That was only the beginning. From July 1 to the end of the season, he won 11 games and lost only three.

With Langston leading the way, the Mariners finished the 1984 season only 10 games behind the American League West champion, the Kansas City Royals. Seattle fans began forecasting a winning season and maybe even a division title in the near future.

However, the fans didn't count on injuries taking their toll on the team's talented young players. In 1985, for example, almost the entire pitching staff went down with

First baseman Bruce Bochte.

Graceful outfielder Phil Bradley.

one ailment or another. "The play I called the most often this year was 'Call the Doctor,'" sighed manager Chuck Cottier.

In 1987 everyone was finally healthy, and the Mariners challenged for the AL West lead nearly the entire season. Langston set a club record by winning 19 games, first baseman Alvin Davis and center fielder Phil Bradley each hit nearly .300, and new second baseman Harold Reynolds led the league in stolen bases. As late as September, the Mariners were still in the hunt for the division title. Then the Minnesota Twins went on a winning streak near the end of the season, and Seattle dropped back to fourth place, seven games behind the Twins.

1989

Second baseman Harold Reynolds won his second consecutive Gold Glove award for his fine defensive play.

Finally, team owner George Argyros became impatient. "The Mariners are no longer an expansion team," he announced. "It's time we began winning." Argyros made several managerial changes over the next two years and traded away such crowd favorites as Mark Langston and Phil Bradley. Mariners fans were upset by the trades, but some of the players who arrived in Seattle as a result—pitcher Randy Johnson and outfielder Jay Buhner—became an important part of the team's success in the 1990s.

FINDING WINNING INGREDIENTS

Always important to a team's success is its leadership. Many fans have credited the Mariners' winning ways in the 1990s to skipper Lou Piniella. Piniella was a longtime outfielder for the New York Yankees before retiring as a player to coach the team from 1986 through 1988. In 1990 he agreed to manage the Cincinnati Reds, leading

All-Star second baseman Harold Reynolds (pages 18-19).

them to a stunning sweep of the Oakland Athletics in the World Series.

In 1993, Piniella moved west to coach the Mariners. Piniella's talent for getting his group of All-Stars to play as a team has made him unique. While some other teams of highly paid players fight and complain, the Mariners have stuck together with the goal of bringing home a championship to Seattle.

1 9 9 0

After being out with an injury for four months, Jay Buhner returned to hit a grand slam on June 1.

But a manager is nothing without good players. One of the biggest reasons for the Mariners' success has been pitcher Randy Johnson. At 6-foot-10, Johnson is big. He is the tallest player in baseball history, thus earning him the nickname "Big Unit." His lanky frame can wind up to unleash a baseball with more power and pop than any other pitcher in the major leagues. From the top of his delivery, Johnson's pitches come down at bewildered batters with frightening velocity. The fact that Johnson can be wild helps, too. Batters fear that Johnson may accidentally hit them with a 99-mile-per-hour fastball, causing them to focus on survival rather than on hitting.

Amazingly, Johnson came to the Mariners through a trade with the Montreal Expos in 1989. The Expos had given up on the Big Unit despite his imposing size and amazing fastball. They thought he was too wild to ever succeed in the majors. In Seattle, Johnson has developed into the most feared starter in baseball. Texas Rangers general manager Doug Melvin offered Johnson high praise, proclaiming that "Randy Johnson has become what [pitching great] Sandy Koufax was."

In addition to successful trades, Seattle used its farm system (minor-league teams) to develop other stars—notably center fielder Ken Griffey Jr., designated hitter Edgar Martinez, and shortstop Alex Rodriguez.

Left-hander Dave Fleming led the club in wins (17), innings pitched (228.1), and ERA (3.39).

JUNIOR JOLTS THE BIG LEAGUES

Few players have made as strong an early impression as Ken Griffey Jr., who arrived in Seattle in 1989 at an incredibly mature 19 years old. "I don't think anybody has ever been that good at that age," said Mariners hitting coach Gene Clines. "He's in his own category. He's a natural."

Griffey hit a double in his first major-league at-bat in Oakland and a home run on the first pitch he saw in the Kingdome a few nights later. He was on his way to a Rookie of

First baseman Tino Martinez.

"Big Unit"—Randy Johnson.

the Year season in 1989 when he fell in late July and broke a finger. When he returned to the lineup a month later, he began pressing too much, and his statistics fell.

However, he was back and better than ever in 1990. He batted more than .300 most of the year and became the first Mariner elected to the starting lineup in the All-Star Game. And on August 31, 1990, he and his father, Ken Griffey Sr., became the first father-son tandem to play in the same major-league lineup.

"Junior," as the younger Ken Griffey is known, plays an excellent all-around game. In fact, Griffey enjoys stopping runs more than scoring them. "I like defense more than offense," he said. "I'd rather run somebody's hit down and then watch them get mad over it. I know that takes something away from the other team and helps us win."

1 9 9 3

Pitcher Chris Bosio tossed a no-hitter in defeating the Boston Red Sox 7–0 on April 23.

Another player who helped the Mariners win was designated hitter Edgar Martinez. The right-handed slugger had slowly worked his way up through the Mariners' farm system, finally making his major-league debut in 1987 after five years in the minors. Because Martinez doesn't have the natural talent of a Ken Griffey Jr., he had learned to work hard at his trade. The work paid off, as Martinez blossomed into one of baseball's deadliest bats. "Edgar has been so consistent for us," said former Mariner manager Jim Lefebvre. "He's a pleasure to watch at the plate."

In 1992, Martinez hit .343 and became the first Mariner to win a batting title. He topped that effort in 1995 by winning his second batting crown, this time with a .356 average. It was the highest season total by a right-handed hitter since Joe DiMaggio hit .381 in 1939. The consistent play of Edgar

Martinez was part of the reason the Mariners reached the 1995 American League playoffs.

1 9 9 4

Ken Griffey Jr. belted 40 home runs to lead the league in the strike-shortened season.

TASTING PLAYOFF SUCCESS

In 1995, the Mariners compiled a 79–66 record, earning them a chance to play the New York Yankees for the division title. The Mariners' playoff inexperience and postseason jitters allowed New York to take a commanding 2–0 lead in the best-of-five series. Game two was particularly disheartening for the excited crew from Seattle, as the Mariners lost on a 15th-inning home run by Yankees catcher Jim Leyritz. The five-hour, twelve-minute contest was the longest postseason game ever played.

Second baseman Mike Blowers.

Despite their disappointment, the Mariners returned to the Kingdome determined to show the Yankees—and the baseball world—that they were a legitimate playoff team. Manager Lou Piniella wisely counted on his ace, Randy Johnson, to turn the tide for Seattle. The Big Unit came through marvelously, pitching a four-hit game to give Seattle the win in front of 57,411 delirious fans.

1 9 9 5

Randy Johnson topped the American League in strikeouts (294) and ERA (2.48).

Game four proved to be even more exciting—and gut-wrenching—for Mariners fans. With the home team down 5–0, Edgar Martinez came alive in the third inning, smashing a three-run homer off Yankees starter Scott Kamieniecki to bring the Mariners back into contention. In the eighth inning, Martinez broke open a 6–6 tie by hitting a grand slam to force the series to a fifth and deciding game.

Having faced elimination and survived, the Mariners could not wait for game five. They got off to a slow start, needing to come from two runs behind in the eighth inning to tie the game. Piniella again turned to Johnson for inspiration, asking if he could pitch some relief on only a day's rest. Johnson responded, pitching scoreless ball in the ninth and 10th innings. In the 11th, however, New York scored a run, leaving Seattle fans concerned that their team's season was about to end. But the Mariners' new-found hero, Edgar Martinez, would not allow the Yankees to spoil his party. In the bottom of the 11th, he drilled a double that scored both Joey Cora and a hustling Ken Griffey Jr., sending the Kingdome fans into ecstasy.

Of his game-five hit, Martinez said, "I thought game four was the greatest game I ever played, but this is the best." Not only had the Mariners reached postseason play for the

Superstar Ken Griffey Jr. (pages 26-27).

first time, they had also beaten the legendary New York Yankees after trailing two games to none. The baseball world took notice.

1 9 9 6

Alex Rodriguez led the league with a .358 average and led all shortstops with 36 home runs.

Next came the powerful Cleveland Indians to battle for the American League championship. Critics gave the Mariners little chance against Cleveland's potent offense with hitters like Kenny Lofton, Albert Belle, Carlos Baerga, and Roberto Alomar. However, surprise game-one starter Bob Wolcott, a 22-year-old rookie, stifled Cleveland's offense, pitching a gritty two-hit gem. Second baseman Luis Sojo won the game with a run-scoring double in the seventh inning to make the final score 3–2. The Mariners had scored an early upset.

Game two was won by Cleveland 5–2 behind the pitching of series MVP Orel Hershiser. In game three, a new star arose in Jay Buhner, who drilled the second of his two home runs in the 11th inning to lead Seattle to 5–2 victory. The Mariners now led the series 2–1 and had proven to the baseball world that their talents were for real. They needed only two more wins to reach the World Series.

In game four, however, the wheels came off of Seattle's playoff bandwagon. They were routed 7–0 in a loss that shook the team's confidence. Seattle dropped the next two games and the series.

Though the season ended with three tough losses, Mariners fans were happy that their team had shown the world they could play with any team in baseball.

The 1996 season started full of promise, but it proved to be a frustrating year. While setting a Seattle record for most wins in a season with 85, the Mariners could never quite reach the top of the standings. Injuries to Griffey and Johnson crippled the team's efforts, and they were never able to recover. The Mariners' hopes in 1996 had sunk. But even though they didn't make the playoffs, they did find a new star with whom to set sail.

1 9 9 7

Edgar Martinez ranked 2nd in the AL in batting average (.330) and on-base percentage (.454).

"A-ROD" BRIGHTENS MARINERS' HOPES

When searching for bright spots in the disappointing 1996 season, Mariners manager Lou Piniella kept finding himself talking about a wiry 20-year-old shortstop by the name of Alex Rodriguez. "A-Rod [Rodriguez] had the best season I've ever seen a player his age have," exclaimed the veteran skipper.

In his first full campaign with Seattle, Rodriguez won the American League batting title with a .358 average. He added 36 home runs, 123 RBIs, and 141 runs scored and became the youngest shortstop ever selected to play in the All-Star Game. Teammate Edgar Martinez expressed admiration for Rodriguez's play. "Alex has become a great player in a short time," observed Martinez. "He can run, throw, and field. He can hit for average and for power. He has handled fame and attention well."

Even players on other teams recognize Rodriguez's talents. In fact, his idol, Baltimore Orioles third baseman Cal Ripken, said, "Alex has a real good chance to be the best shortstop ever." From a man whom many consider to presently hold that title, that is high praise indeed.

Tough left-handed starter Jeff Fassero.

Versatile infielder Rich Amaral.

1 9 9 8

Having hit a career-high 11 home runs the previous year, Joey Cora was anticipating another fine season.

With Rodriguez hooking up with a healthy Randy Johnson and Ken Griffey Jr., the Mariners took off in 1997, winning 90 games and recapturing the Al West title. Griffey led the way with an incredible 56-homer, 147-RBI season, clinching his first AL MVP award. In the postseason, however, the Mariners fell to the hard-hitting Baltimore Orioles. But even in a losing effort, Rodriguez found positives. "It always hurts to lose, but we're still a young team, and I think our time is coming soon."

The Mariners definitely have championship caliber weapons. Griffey, Rodriguez, and Martinez, along with slugging right fielder Jay Buhner, look to form baseball's most powerful lineup into the 21st century. In 1997, Seattle's sluggers set a major-league record for home runs in a season by a team, with 264.

On the pitching side, the Mariners' starting staff features Johnson and fellow lefties Jeff Fassero and Jamie Moyer. The threesome combined in 1997 to win more games (53) than any other rotation trio in the American League. "We have what everybody wants—great left-handed pitching," Piniella said with a grin. "If we can find a guy to close the show, we're going to be a handful." The team has high hopes that relievers Heathcliff Slocumb, Bobby Ayala, and Mike Timlin can take care of the late innings for the club in the future.

With a galaxy of stars lighting up their roster, Seattle's days at the bottom of the league standings should be over. It seems these Mariners are prepared to set sail for their first World Series title.